Dedicated to Uncle Roy,
Auntie Joy, Valisa Higman,
and the town of Seldovia, Alaska,
the inspirations for this story.

Library of Congress Cataloging-in-Publication Data available

ISBN 978-1-338-61799-3

10 9 8 7 6 5 4 3 2 1   20 21 22 23 24
Printed in the U.S.A.   76

This edition first printing 2020

Grumpycorn

By Sarah McIntyre

Scholastic Inc.

Unicorn was sitting in his special writing house.

"I am going to write the most fabulous story in the world," he thought.

This made him feel very pleased with himself.
He already liked being a writer.

But Unicorn didn't know where to begin his story.

"I need my special fluffy PEN," he said.

He went and got his special fluffy pen.

But . . .

. . . he didn't know what to write.

"I need a cup of my special moonberry TEA," he said. "Then I will be able to write my story."

He went and made himself a cup of his special moonberry tea.

And Unicorn sat at his desk, wondering what to write in his special fancy notebook.

He sighed.

"I wish an idea would come knocking at my door."

But Narwhal knocked instead.
"What are you doing, Unicorn?"

"I am busy writing the most
fabulous story in the world!"
said Unicorn.

"WOW!" said Narwhal.
"Can I be in your story?"

"Don't be **silly**," said Unicorn. "No one wants to read a story about a narwhal. Narwhals are very boring. There will be no narwhals in my story."

"Oh," said Narwhal. He swam sadly away.

"Mermaid, guess what?" said Narwhal.
"Unicorn is writing the most fabulous
story in the world!"

Mermaid looked impressed.
She swam off to visit Unicorn.
"Hello, Unicorn!" she said. "How is
your story coming along?"

"Very badly," said Unicorn.
"I am waiting for my Moment of Genius.

"And . . . I do not have any cookies. My genius ideas will
only come to me if I can get some cookies to eat."

Mermaid had an idea.
"If I bake you
cookies . . . can I
be in your story?"

Unicorn thought for a moment.
"MAYBE . . . but only if the cookies make me feel inspired."

Mermaid swam back to her submarine to bake her famous starfish cookies. Narwhal helped. He loved licking the bowl.

Mermaid brought the cookies to Unicorn.
"Now can I be in your story?" she asked.

Unicorn took a bite of cookie and looked thoughtful.

He ate the whole plate of cookies and kept looking thoughtful.

"No," said Unicorn. "I'm afraid you can't be in my story. They were very good cookies, but they did not **inspire** me."

Mermaid swam away
in a huff.

"What's wrong,
Mermaid?"
asked Jellyfish.

"Unicorn is writing the most
fabulous story in the **world**,"
she sniffed. "But he won't let me
be in it! My cookies were not
inspiring enough."

"Maybe I'M in it?" said Jellyfish.
"Everyone loves jellyfish."
She wriggled with excitement and
swam off to visit Unicorn.

"Hello, Unicorn!" said Jellyfish. "Have you finished your fabulous story yet? I can't **wait** to read it! Is there a jellyfish in it?

"Why don't you let **me** be in your story? I will be the most brave jellyfish and go into space and discover fantastic alien jellyfish and . . ."

"**NOOOOOOOOOOOO!**"

howled Unicorn. "I can't get ANY ideas because everyone keeps bothering me! You are all very silly and annoying and I don't want to write this story ANYMORE!"

"Oh, what a GRUMPYCORN!" said Jellyfish.

Unicorn threw his fluffy pen, his notebook, and his teacup into the sea.

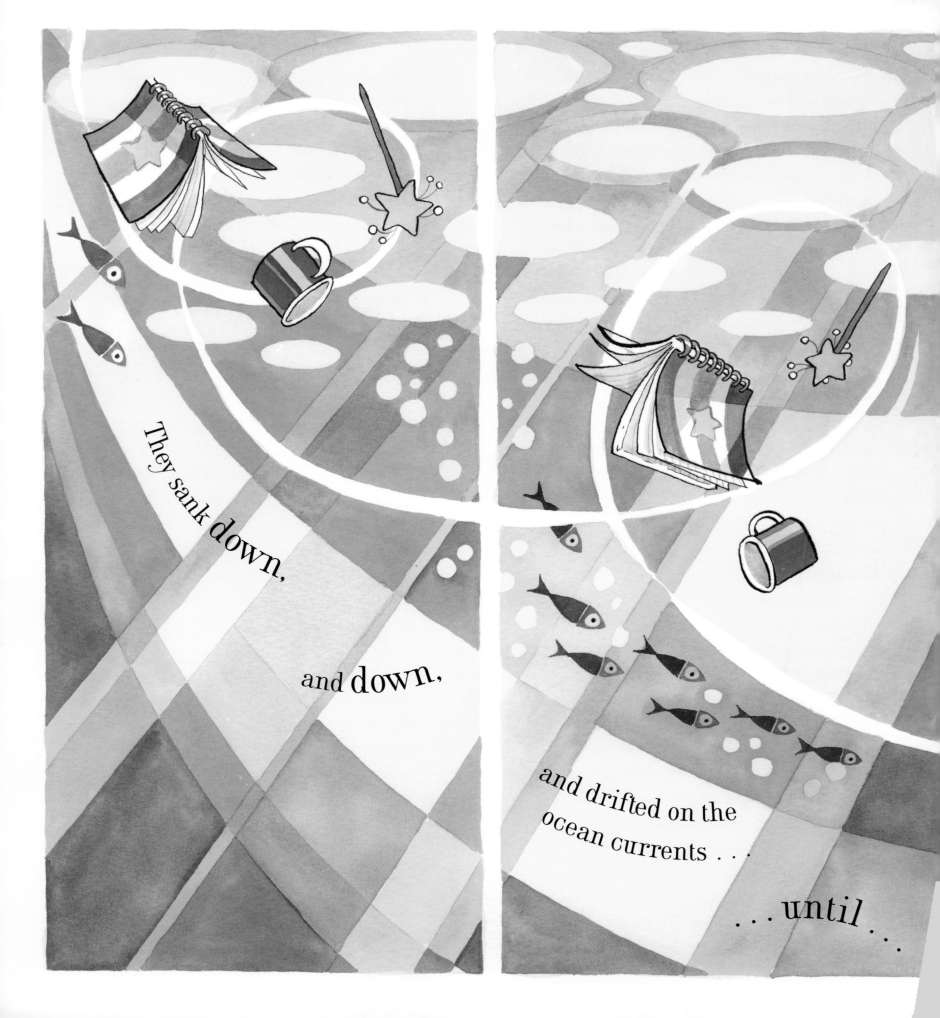

They sank down,

and down,

and drifted on the ocean currents . . .

. . . until . . .

"Look!" said Mermaid.
"It's the most FABULOUS story
in the world!"
"Yippee! Let's read it!"
said Narwhal.

The friends gathered around to read Unicorn's story.
But . . . Unicorn had not written a single word.
"Poor Grumpycorn," said Mermaid. "I wish we could help."

"I have an idea!" said Narwhal.

Once upon a time
a unicorn tried to
write the most
FABULOUS
story in the world

"He was visited by a **world-famous** baker!" said Mermaid.

"And the **bravest** jellyfish in the ocean . . ." said Jellyfish.

"And the **cleverest** narwhal in the whole universe," agreed Narwhal.

A few hours later, Unicorn arrived,
carrying a big flat box.
"I tried to write a fabulous story," he said.
"But I was not a very fabulous friend.

"But I AM fabulous at ordering pizza!
I brought this to say I'm sorry."
"That looks like very INSPIRING pizza!" said Narwhal.
"And you are JUST in time . . ."

"... to help us finish the most **amazing**, **clever**, **fabulous**, and **funny**...

...story
in the
WORLD!"